P9-BYN-204

OTHER YEARLING BOOKS YOU WILL ENJOY
by Patricia Reilly Giff
illustrated by Blanche Sims

YEARLING BOOKS/YOUNG YEARLINGS/YEARLING CLASSICS are designed especially to entertain and enlighten young people. Patricia Reilly Giff, consultant to this series, received her bachelor's degree from Marymount College and a master's degree in history from St. John's University. She holds a Professional Diploma in Reading and a Doctorate of Humane Letters from Hofstra University. She was a teacher and reading consultant for many years, and is the author of numerous books for young readers.

For a complete listing of all Yearling titles,
write to Dell Readers Service,
P.O. Box 1045, South Holland, IL 60473.

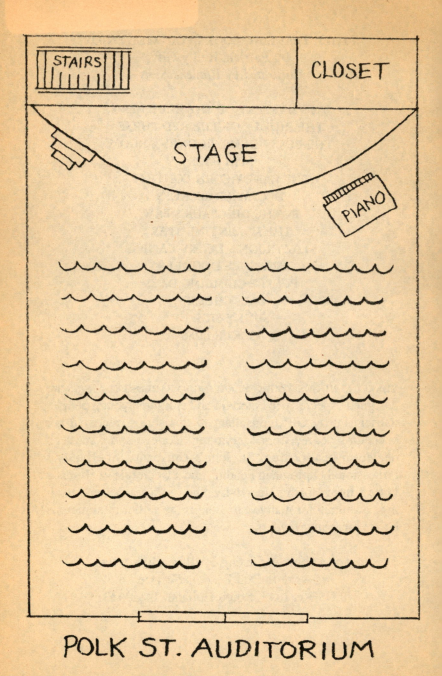

STAIRS

CLOSET

STAGE

PIANO

POLK ST. AUDITORIUM

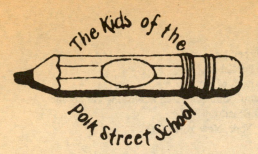

The Kids of the Polk Street School

THE SECRET AT THE POLK STREET SCHOOL

Patricia Reilly Giff

Illustrated by Blanche Sims

A YOUNG YEARLING BOOK

Published by
Dell Publishing
a division of
Bantam Doubleday Dell Publishing Group, Inc.
1540 Broadway
New York, New York 10036

If you purchased this book without a cover you should be aware that this book is stolen property. It was reported as "unsold and destroyed" to the publisher and neither the author nor the publisher has received any payment for this "stripped book."

Text copyright © 1987 by Patricia Reilly Giff

Illustrations copyright © 1987 by Blanche Sims

All rights reserved. No part of this book may be reproduced or transmitted in any form or by any means, electronic or mechanical, including photocopying, recording, or by any information storage and retrieval system, without the written permission of the Publisher, except where permitted by law.

The trademark Yearling® is registered in the U.S. Patent and Trademark Office.

The Trademark Dell® is registered in the U.S. Patent and Trademark Office.

ISBN: 0-440-47696-8

Printed in the United States of America

November 1987

20 19 18 17 16

CWO

With admiration
to my favorite professor:
Dr. Sidney Rauch

···CHAPTER ONE···

Dawn Bosco took big steps.

Her cowgirl boots went *click-clack*.

Jason was click-clacking, too. He had robot boots.

They went into the school yard.

Dawn opened her mouth. "Spring is springing," she sang. "Grass is ringing."

Jason started to laugh. "That's not right."

1

Dawn laughed, too. "I like the way it sounds."

Drake Evans was kneeling near the picnic table.

He was poking around in the dirt.

"You sound like my dog howling," he told Dawn. He put his nose in the air. "Aaooow!"

"Don't pay attention," Jason said.

"I won't," said Dawn.

Drake Evans was the meanest boy in the school. Everyone knew that.

Dawn was glad he was in Mrs. Gates's class and not in Ms. Rooney's.

In the classroom Dawn put her books away. She made a skinny point on her pencil.

"Happy spring," Ms. Rooney said. She clapped her hands. "Is everybody ready? It's idea time."

Dawn reached into her pocket. She pulled out a piece of paper.

It was a little wrinkled.

She smoothed it out.

"Who has an idea for us?" Ms. Rooney asked.

Dawn put her hand up.

Emily's hand went up, too. So did Richard's and Timothy Barbiero's.

"Yes, Richard," said Ms. Rooney.

"We want to win the banner," Richard said. "Right?"

"Right-a-reeno," said Matthew. "I hope Mr. Mancina gives it to us."

Mr. Mancina was the principal.

This week he was giving the banner to a special class. It was the class that did the most for the school.

The banner was blue and white.

It had long gold strings.

3

It said BEST.

Ms. Rooney's class wanted to be the best. They hadn't had the banner in a long time.

"My idea is"—Richard took a deep breath —"we could paint the hall."

"That would be doing something good for the school," said Matthew.

"It would be some mess!" said Emily Arrow.

"It's a mess now," said Richard. "All brown and tan."

"I'd like a red hall," said Matthew.

"Me, too," said Jason. "Or orange."

Richard sat up on his desk. "How about stripes?"

Sometimes Richard had good ideas, Dawn thought.

She still thought hers was better.

Everyone was looking at Ms. Rooney.

Everyone was yelling a different color for the hall.

Ms. Rooney was smiling. "It's not practical," she said.

Ms. Rooney always said that, thought Dawn. That meant it wasn't a good idea.

Dawn waved her hand harder.

"Let's listen to Dawn's idea," said Ms. Rooney.

Dawn read her idea paper. "Everyone knows I'm a great detective." She looked around. "Right?"

Linda Lorca made a face.

"You're the best," said Jason.

Dawn reached into her desk.

She pulled out her polka dot detective hat. She pushed it up on her head.

It was a little big.

"We could find a mystery," she said. "I could solve it."

5

"That would help the school," said Jason.

"You could say that again," Richard said. "Got you, thief."

Matthew gave Richard a punch. "Let the thief have my homework."

They started to laugh.

"That's better than my sister's class. They're having a bake sale," Jason said. "My sister's a terrible baker."

Dawn nodded. She was thrilled. Her idea was great.

She tried not to smile.

"No good," said Linda Lorca.

Dawn made a face at her. Sometimes Linda looked like a horse. "Why not?" she asked.

Linda raised one shoulder. "We don't have a mystery."

"Neigh." Dawn made a horse noise under her breath.

Ms. Rooney smiled. "Mysteries always come along."

Ms. Rooney looked at Timothy. "How about you, Tim?"

Dawn sat down.

She ripped up her idea paper.

She didn't even listen to Timothy's idea.

It probably wasn't practical.

Everyone started to clap.

They liked Timothy's idea. Even Ms. Rooney.

It was probably silly, Dawn thought.

She looked out the window.

She'd find a mystery all by herself.

· · · CHAPTER TWO · · ·

On Tuesday they started to work on Timothy's idea.

It wasn't a bad idea, thought Dawn.

Not bad at all.

It would be a great surprise for the school.

Dawn walked across the stage.

She took little baby steps.

9

She had a cake box in one hand.

She had a can of chicken soup in the other.

A loaf of bread was tucked under her arm.

It was quiet on the stage.

Very quiet.

She was all alone up there.

Then she heard something.

Swish. Swish.

She looked over her shoulder.

Her red hood fell down over her eyes. She pushed it back.

She tried to walk faster.

Someone was coming from the side of the stage.

She looked again.

She saw hands. They had long pointy fingernails.

She saw a face. Hair was growing all over it.

"I'm going to get you!" the voice whispered.

It was a terrible voice.

Dawn screamed as loud as she could.

Ms. Rooney was sitting in the front row. She clapped her hands. "Wait a minute," she said.

"That's all wrong," said Linda Lorca. Linda was sitting at the piano. "The wolf isn't supposed to say that."

"And Red Riding Hood doesn't scream," said Emily.

"I hope my idea doesn't get wrecked," Timothy said. "This play has to be a good one."

Dawn put the cake box on the floor.

She put the bread on top of it.

She put her hands on her hips.

She looked at the wolf.

"How come you tried to scare me, Jason?" she asked.

The wolf disappeared behind the curtain.

"Jason?" Dawn asked.

Jason didn't answer.

"Some wolf you are," Dawn told him.

"Jason," Ms. Rooney called.

Jason still didn't answer.

Ms. Rooney stood up.

Dawn went to the back of the stage.

No one was there.

"Hey!" she said.

She went out front again. "He's not there."

In back of the auditorium the doors opened.

Everyone turned around.

It was Jason.

He wiped his mouth on his sleeve. "I had to get a drink."

He marched down the aisle.

Dawn's mouth opened.

How did Jason get back there so fast?

One minute he had been on the stage. The next minute he was in the hall.

She blinked.

"You did the wolf part wrong," Sherri Dent told him.

"You didn't even growl a little," said Matthew. He made a wolf face. "Grrr."

"I didn't even do the wolf part yet," said Jason. He crossed his eyes at them. "I'm the best growler in the class."

He went up the stage steps on his hands and knees. "Yuff yiff. Ai ai ai."

Jason was right, Dawn thought. He was a terrific growler.

Jason looked around. "Where's my wolf suit? Where are my fake fingernails?"

Dawn helped him look. "Where did you take them off?"

"I didn't put them on yet," he said.

Linda Lorca stuck out her lip. "Those fingers took a long time to make. You'd better find them."

"Neigh," said Dawn under her breath.

Jason crawled to the edge of the stage. He looked worried. "My sister Peggy will kill me. She doesn't know I took her wolf suit."

Ms. Rooney clapped her hands again. "It's too late to start now," she said. "It's almost time to go home."

The class lined up.

Dawn kept thinking about the wolf suit.

She thought about the long fingernails.

She thought about the voice. "I'm going to get you," it had said.

She looked behind her.

"Are you sure it wasn't you?" she asked Jason.

"Cross my toes," he said.

They went into the classroom.

Dawn wished she were home. She didn't want to tell anyone she was afraid.

She was a detective.

Detectives weren't supposed to be afraid.

She could feel a lump of worry in her chest.

She wondered what would happen next.

$\cdots$ CHAPTER THREE $\cdots$

It was after school.
"Wait for me!" Dawn called to Jason.
She went into the auditorium.
She looked around.
Her red riding cape was on a chair.
She hoped no one had seen it.
The play was a surprise.

She went outside.

She and Jason stopped at the corner.

She wanted to show Carmen, the school crossing guard, how she looked.

Carmen wouldn't tell anyone about the play.

Carmen blew her whistle. "Pretty nifty," she said.

"We're doing *Red Riding Hood*," Dawn said.

Jason hopped up and down on the curb. "We're going to surprise the school."

"Don't tell anyone," said Dawn.

"Not a soul," Carmen said. She went to the middle of the street. "Watch out for the wolf," she called back.

Jason nodded. "That's what I say."

Dawn and Jason crossed the street.

Dawn looked over her shoulder. "It wasn't a real wolf," she said. "I know that."

"It was a person," said Jason. "He was dressed in my sister Peggy's wolf suit."

"A big person, I think," said Dawn. "A person with a scary voice."

She could feel her lips moving.

Maybe she was going to cry.

She hoped not.

She put her hand up so Jason couldn't see.

Jason thought for a minute. "He couldn't have been so big."

Dawn frowned. "Why not?"

"He was wearing Peggy's suit."

Dawn crossed her fingers. "I knew that all along."

"I hope Peggy doesn't go down to the basement," Jason said. "I hope she doesn't look for her wolf suit."

"Maybe she won't," said Dawn.

Drake Evans was walking ahead of them.

"Arf, arf," he said when he saw Dawn.

Dawn made believe she didn't hear him.

Drake's friend Louie was with him.

Louie was loud.

Louie was big.

Louie was mean.

He was even meaner than Drake Evans.

They were skipping stones across the street.

"You're not supposed to throw stones," Dawn said.

"Dog voice," Drake told her.

"Dog face," Louie said.

Dawn put her tongue out.

Jason did a wolf growl.

Then they started to run.

They stopped on the next street.

"Whew!" said Dawn.

"I just thought of something," said Jason.

Dawn clicked her cowgirl boots. "What?"

Jason scratched his knee. "Itchy," he said. He looked back at Drake and Louie. "Maybe one of them . . ."

"One of them what?"

"Maybe one of them was the wolf."

Dawn looked back, too.

"You think Drake wore your wolf suit?"

"Maybe," said Jason. "And my fake fingernails."

Dawn shivered. "You think Drake is going to get me?"

"I hope not," said Jason. "It's a mystery."

Dawn didn't answer. She knew Jason was looking at her.

He was waiting.

She took a breath.

She opened her mouth.

"I'm the Polka Dot Private Eye," she said. "I'm the one who solves mysteries."

"That's what I was thinking," said Jason.

"I'll solve this mystery, too," said Dawn. "I'll call it The Secret at the Polk Street School."

CHAPTER FOUR

"Don't say a word," Dawn whispered.

"Don't even breathe," said Jason.

They were at Drake Evans's house.

They were kneeling behind the bushes.

It was muddy back there.

Dawn could feel her good jeans getting wet.

She tried to kneel on one knee.

One clean knee was better than two dirty ones, she thought.

Jason tapped her arm. "I hear them coming."

They ducked down.

Dawn's clean knee dug into the mud.

Drake had a pile of cookies in his mouth.

So did Louie.

Louie stepped in a puddle. Water went over Drake's jeans.

"Hey!" Drake said. He opened his mouth wide. It looked like sawdust inside.

Louie started to laugh.

Cookies sprayed all over the place.

"Yuck," Dawn whispered.

Drake stopped chewing. "What was that noise?"

Louie raised one shoulder. "The cat. A bird. Who cares?"

Drake and Louie sat down on the steps.

Drake leaned over. He said something to Louie.

Behind the bushes, Dawn tried to hear. She moved closer.

She could feel her knees squish.

"We did it!" said Drake.

"Yup," said Louie.

"Did what?" Jason said to Dawn.

"Sh!" Dawn said.

"Where did you put . . ." Drake began. He put a cookie into his mouth.

"In the auditorium," said Louie. "In the stage closet."

Jason and Dawn looked at each other.

Dawn nodded.

Just then, Drake leaned over the bushes.

He saw Dawn looking up at him. "Spies!" he yelled. "Let's go, men!"

Louie stopped. He put a cookie into his mouth.

Then he jumped off the steps, too.

Dawn slid out from behind the bushes. The branches stuck into her cape.

She ran across the lawn.

Jason ran after her.

"Get them!" Drake shouted.

Dawn ran down the street. She went as fast as she could.

Jason was running, too. He was right behind her.

She could hear him taking big breaths.

Drake came next.

Louie pounded after him.

At the corner Dawn ran one way. Jason went the other.

"Which way?" yelled Louie.

"You get her!" shouted Drake. "I'll get Jason."

Dawn reached the A&P. She pushed open the doors.

She ran down the aisle.

"Excuse me," she said to a lady with a shopping cart.

She dashed around her.

She looked over her shoulder.

Louie was behind her. He was stuck in back of the lady with the cart.

The lady was reaching for a can of peaches.

Dawn dived around the corner.

She hid behind a stack of cereal boxes.

Louie ran past her.

Dawn waited a minute. Then another.

She peeked out.

The lady with the cart reached for a box of Krispies.

She jumped when she saw Dawn.

"Excuse me," Dawn said.

She looked around the lady.

Louie was gone.

Dawn tiptoed down the aisle. She passed the frozen foods.

She stopped to see if they had any orange ice.

It was her favorite.

There were a zillion boxes in the freezer.

Too bad she didn't have any money.

She looked out the window. Sherri Dent's mother was talking with Mrs. Arrow outside.

No one else was around.

She went outside.

She hoped Jason was all right. She wondered where he went.

For a minute she stood there.

There was something she had to do.

She had to go back to school.

Too bad it was getting dark. The street lights were on. It was almost suppertime.

She was a detective.

She couldn't even cry.

··· CHAPTER FIVE ···

The wind was blowing. It had gotten colder.

Dawn put her hands into her cape pockets.

A pack of gum was in one pocket. A piece of paper was in the other.

Dawn turned in at the school-yard gate.

No one was in the yard. Everyone had gone home.

She hoped she could still get into school.

She pulled on the handle. "Whew!" she said. The door was open.

It was good to get inside. Everything looked different, though.

The lights were on.

There was no noise.

She could hear Ms. Rooney in the office. She and Mrs. Gates were laughing.

Dawn loved to hear Ms. Rooney's laugh. It had a nice "ha-ha" sound.

Dawn tiptoed past the office. If Ms. Rooney saw her, she'd be in trouble.

The door to the auditorium was closed.

She opened it quietly. It always squeaked.

The lights were off. She could just about see the seats.

The stage curtain looked black instead of blue.

She went down the aisle. She had to see what Drake had put in the closet.

She bet it was the wolf suit. And the fake nails, too.

It was really dark on the stage.

She couldn't find the closet door.

She reached around the wall with her hands.

Then she felt the knob.

The door swung open.

Inside it was black.

Dawn blinked. She couldn't see a thing.

She heard Ms. Rooney call, "Good-night, Clara."

The outside door banged open and shut.

Dawn stepped away from the closet.

She was ready to run.

"Don't do that," she told herself. "Be brave."

She opened her mouth. She started to

sing: "Don't be afraid. Be brave as a wave. Brave as a cave."

She put her hand into the closet.

"Plain air," she sang. "Not a bear."

She took a step inside.

There was stuff on the floor. She felt around.

There should be a wolf suit somewhere.

There should be fingernails, too.

No. Just some old tools.

The door slammed shut.

She pushed it hard.

It wouldn't open.

"Yeow!" she yelled. "Noni, save me!"

She pushed again.

"Let me out! Drake? Louie?"

No one answered.

She put her ear against the door.

She couldn't hear anything. Not one thing.

She sank down on the floor.

There were probably spider webs.

Spiders, too.

She'd have to stay in there all night.

No dinner.

No bed.

She was starving. All she had was some gum.

Her grandmother, Noni, would look for her.

She'd never find her, though.

Dawn couldn't even cry. Detectives don't cry.

She leaned against the door.

Then she heard something.

Footsteps.

Maybe it was Drake or Louie.

Suppose it was someone else?

Maybe someone was going to get her.
She backed up against the closet wall.
The footsteps were louder.
They were click-clacking.
She began to scream.

···CHAPTER SIX···

The door banged open.

"I've got a gun!" Dawn yelled.

"Don't be silly," said Jason. "I thought you were brave."

"Of course I'm brave," Dawn said. She stepped out of the closet.

"It wasn't even locked," Jason said.

"I pushed," Dawn said. "I pushed hard."

Jason laughed. "You have to turn the knob."

Dawn laughed a little, too. She didn't feel like laughing, though.

They started across the stage.

"Be very quiet," Jason said. "Jim is sweeping. We're not supposed to be in here."

Dawn stopped. "How did you find me?"

Jason took a breath. "I got away from Drake. I climbed a tree. He went right past me."

Jason swung off the stage. "I could have jumped down on top of him. Pow."

"Sh," said Dawn. "Not so loud."

"I'm glad Louie didn't get you," Jason said.

"Not me." Dawn made a fist. "Double pow."

They hurried down the aisle.

They opened the auditorium door.

It made a loud squeak.

Jim was sweeping at the end of the hall.

They started to run.

Jim banged his broom on the floor. "Hey, you two!"

They looked at each other. They slowed down.

"Dawn Bosco," Jim said. "Jason Bazyk. What are you doing?"

"I was looking for something," Dawn said.

"How about you?" Jim asked Jason.

"I knew Dawn was looking for something," Jason said. "I thought she needed help."

"How did you know I was there?" Dawn asked again.

"I remembered what Louie said. I knew you'd go and look."

Jim swept the dirt into the dustpan. "What will Ms. Rooney say?"

"Don't tell," said Jason.

"Please," said Dawn.

Jim stopped to think.

"You have to promise—"

"We promise," Dawn said.

"—never to come to school this late," Jim said.

"We won't," said Jason.

"Never again," said Dawn.

They went outside.

"I'm going to get killed," Jason said. "I'm supposed to do homework."

"Me, too," said Dawn.

She reached into her pocket. "Want some gum?"

She pulled everything out.

Two sticks of gum.

A piece of paper.

Jason took a stick of gum. "What's that paper?"

Dawn put some gum into her mouth. "My homework? A shopping list?"

She opened the paper.

She stopped chewing.

She waved the paper around. "Listen!" she said.

Jason sat down on the curb. "My robot boots are beginning to hurt."

Dawn sat down next to him. "This isn't a shopping list. It isn't homework."

"What is it?"

"It's a letter."

Jason pulled off one boot. "A stone."

Dawn began to read: " 'Dawn Bosco. I'm going to get you. Jason, too.' "

Jason put his boot back on. "Who's it from?" he asked.

Dawn raised one shoulder in the air. "I don't know," she said. "It's signed, 'The Wolf.'"

···CHAPTER SEVEN···

It was Wednesday morning.

It was time to work on the play.

Dawn was up on the stage. She was sitting behind the blue curtain.

She had on her red riding cape.

Jason was sitting next to her.

He was wearing a new wolf suit.

It was Jill Simon's fake fur rug.

It was a mess.

"You have to hurry," Jason told Dawn. "You have to solve the mystery."

He made a face. "I don't want Peggy to know about her wolf suit."

Dawn looked out of the curtain.

Richard was fooling with Matthew.

They were pushing up the seats.

They sat down on them hard.

"Bam!" said Matthew.

"Double bam!" said Richard.

"Triple bam!" said Ms. Rooney. "You'll never win the banner this way."

Ms. Rooney looked at Linda. "Go ahead," she said.

Linda sat down at the piano. She was going to do a song for the play.

She took up almost the whole seat.

"Horse face," Dawn said under her breath.

Linda began to play.

She kept making mistakes.

She kept saying, "Wait."

She started over.

"We won't win the banner this way," said Jason.

"Horrible playing," said Dawn.

Dawn pulled the wolf note out of her pocket.

"I used my detective box last night," she told Jason.

"What did you find out?"

Dawn raised one shoulder. "I looked with my magnifying glass."

"What did you see?"

"Nothing." She put the paper up to her nose. "It smells funny."

Jason leaned over.

He sniffed at the paper.

"I know that smell," he said.

"What is it?"

He tried to think. "I can't remember. It's something horrible."

Dawn held it up to her nose again. "It doesn't smell horrible to me. It smells like flowers or something."

Outside, Linda Lorca stopped playing.

"Try it again," said Ms. Rooney.

Dawn and Jason went to the back of the stage. The closet door was locked.

They went to the little window on the stairs. They looked outside.

"Hey!" said Dawn. "There goes Mrs. Gates's class."

"Drake is carrying a shovel," said Jason.

Dawn thought for a minute. "There was a shovel in the closet," she said.

Jason nodded. "Louie said he put something in the closet."

Dawn bit at her lip. "Just an old shovel?"

she said. "He wasn't talking about the wolf suit."

"I guess not," said Jason.

Dawn took a breath. "Do you know what that means?"

"Drake isn't the wolf," said Jason.

"No," said Dawn.

She watched Mrs. Gates's class. She didn't want to think about the wolf.

Mrs. Gates's class stopped at the picnic table.

Drake stood on top of the table. He started to say something.

He waved his arms around.

"Ms. Rooney would never let us do that," Dawn said.

They heard Ms. Rooney clap her hands.

They ran back to the stage.

Dawn picked up her can of soup. She picked up the bread.

Someone had taken a big bite out of it.

"Gross!" said Dawn.

"It was probably Richard," said Jason. "He likes to fool around."

Dawn looked at the bread. "There are pointy teeth marks in it," she said. "Huge ones."

"Maybe a dog," Jason said.

"Maybe," said Dawn.

Jason looked a little worried. "Maybe . . ."

Dawn pulled up her hood. "Don't say it."

"I won't," said Jason.

Ms. Rooney clapped her hands. "Goodness," she said. "Where's Red Riding Hood? Where's the wolf?"

Dawn opened the curtain.

She stepped out.

"I'm going to my grandmother's house," she said in a loud voice.

Ms. Rooney clapped her hands. "You forgot something."

Dawn didn't say anything.

"Where's your loaf of bread for Granny?" asked Ms. Rooney.

"It's behind the curtain," Dawn said.

She didn't want to touch it.

She didn't even want to look at it.

···CHAPTER EIGHT···

It was lunchtime.

Dawn and Jason walked downstairs together.

"Don't worry," said Jason. "It wasn't a wolf."

Dawn thought about the teeth marks in the bread.

Those horrible teeth marks.

"Detectives aren't afraid," she told herself.

She took a breath. "I know," she told Jason. "It was a person. Someone was trying to scare me."

"Me, too," said Jason.

Dawn frowned. "Why does someone want to scare us?"

Jason put his shoulders in the air.

They stopped outside the cafeteria.

Today was Mrs. Smith's bake sale.

They had set up a table.

In front was a sign.

HELP US WIN THE BANNER.

SMALL COOKIES . . . 5¢

LARGE COOKIES . . . 10¢

MONEY FOR THE SCHOOL

TO BUY A STATUE

OF

JAMES K. POLK

"Yuck," said Jason. "Who wants that?"

Jason's sister Peggy was behind the table. She looked at Jason. "Dummy. Everybody does. Mrs. Smith said so."

Jason gave Dawn a tap. "Don't buy the chocolate chips."

"They look good," Dawn said.

Jason held his fingers to his nose. "My sister made them. She burned the bottoms. My mother had to scrape them off."

Peggy put her hands on her hips.

"Bunny brain," she said to Jason. "Be quiet."

"I'll take an oatmeal cookie," said Dawn.

Peggy sniffed. She put the smallest one in a napkin. "Ten cents."

"A nickel," Dawn said.

Peggy picked up a crumb. She popped it into her mouth. "Wrong, Red Riding Hood. This is big enough for you."

Dawn put out her lip. "No fair."

"Too bad. Put it back if you don't want it."

Mrs. Smith came along. "I see you have a nice big oatmeal cookie." She smiled at Dawn.

Dawn put the dime on the table.

She marched into the cafeteria.

"My sister's tough," Jason said. "Even my father says so."

They each took a tray.

Today was vegetable soup.

It was red. It had squashed peas. It had corn, too.

Dawn hated it.

They sat at the last table.

Drake and Louie were sitting across the way. They were blowing straws at each other.

She kept watching them.

Drake wasn't the wolf.

Neither was Louie.

She picked up her spoon.

She took the peas out of her soup.

She lined them up on her tray.

"Hey!" she said.

"Don't you like those peas?" Jason reached for them.

"Listen!" Dawn said. "I think I know. I know who the wolf is."

"Tell me," Jason said.

Dawn nodded. "I need your help."

···CHAPTER NINE···

Dawn knocked on Jason's side door.

A minute later, he opened it.

He was eating bread and peanut butter. It was all over his mouth.

"Come on in," he said. "I'll make you some."

Dawn went into the kitchen.

The bread was on the table.

So was the knife.

Jason stuck his finger into the peanut butter. He licked it off.

"Hand me the bread," he said.

Yuck, Dawn thought. "Never mind," she said.

"You don't like peanut butter?" Jason put his finger into the jar again.

His sister Peggy came into the kitchen. "Stop doing that," she said. "It's gross."

"Stop bossing me," Jason said.

"Stop fighting!" Jason's mother called.

Peggy picked up the peanut butter. She put the lid on top. "I'm taking this."

"You are not," said Jason.

"I need it for cookies," said Peggy.

Jason grabbed for the jar.

Peggy kicked his leg.

"Yeow!" he yelled.

Mrs. Bazyk came into the kitchen. "What's going on?"

"Tomorrow's the last day," Peggy said. "Holly and I are making cookies."

She looked at Jason. "This elephant won't let me go."

"Jason." Mrs. Bazyk frowned.

Dawn frowned, too. "Let her go."

Peggy pushed past Jason. "I have to hurry. My class wants to win the banner."

She slammed out the door.

"I need coffee." Mrs. Bazyk put a pot onto the stove. "Do you fight with your brother?" she asked Dawn.

Dawn shook her head. "Uh-uh." She crossed her fingers.

They went into the playroom. It had a bunch of clothes on one chair. It had a pile of papers on the other.

Jason threw the papers onto the floor. He sat down.

"Did you forget?" Dawn asked.

He blinked. "Yes. Let's go."

"Going down to the basement!" he called to his mother.

"Why?" she called back.

Jason looked at Dawn. "Just to go down there."

Mrs. Bazyk didn't answer.

They went down the stairs.

Dawn sniffed. It smelled like wet clothes.

"Not much light." Jason hopped down the last step.

Dawn looked around.

It was a good thing she was a detective.

This was a scary place.

"Over here," said Jason. He pointed to some shelves.

He pulled a box down.

Dawn pulled one down, too.

Halloween costumes. A skeleton. A pumpkin.

Dawn pulled out another box.

She put her hand in.

Then she sat back. "Look at this," she told Jason.

Jason reached into the box. "I don't believe it."

Dawn nodded. "It's true," she said.

···CHAPTER TEN···

"Peggy," said Dawn.

"Peggy?" Linda Lorca asked.

"Peggy?" said Richard.

"My own sister," said Jason. "The wolf."

Ms. Rooney's class was standing behind the curtain.

Outside, the whole school was waiting.

"Hurry," said Emily Arrow. "Tell us!"

Jason was wearing Peggy's wolf suit.

He held out his arms.

"We found it in the basement," said Dawn. "Peggy had put it back."

"I don't get it," said Linda.

"I didn't either," Dawn said. "Until the bake sale."

She picked up the can of soup.

She put the bread under her arm.

"Peggy called me Red Riding Hood," she said.

"So?" asked Linda.

"The play was a surprise," said Dawn. "How did she know I was Red Riding Hood?"

"That's right," said Emily. "How *did* she know?"

"I asked her last night," Jason said. "She was up on the stage. She had to get something for Mrs. Smith."

"She saw the wolf suit?" Richard said. "She put it on?"

Jason nodded. He knelt down on the stage. "Yip, yip," he growled. "She was mad. She didn't know I took it."

"You should have asked," said Linda.

"Then she saw my Red Riding cape," said Dawn. "It was on a seat. She put the wolf note in it."

"A scary one," said Jason.

"She made teeth marks in the bread," said Emily.

"With a peanut butter knife," Jason said.

"Peggy wanted to scare us." Dawn put on her Red Riding Hood cape. "She didn't want us to win the banner."

"We'll win," said Jason. "Just watch."

"Is everybody ready?" Ms. Rooney called.

Dawn reached into her cape.

There was a paper in the pocket.

She pulled it out.

"Sorry," it said. "Good luck."

It was signed, "Peggy the Wolf."

Linda sat down at the piano. "I hope I can do this," she said.

The curtain opened.

"I'm going to see my grandmother." Dawn said it in a nice loud voice.

At the same time Linda started to play.

"Oops!" Dawn said. She ran behind the curtain.

Linda made only eight mistakes.

Then Dawn came out again.

The rest of the play was good, Dawn thought.

Everyone clapped.

Even Ms. Rooney.

Mr. Mancina came up on the stage.

"Wonderful," he said.

"Who gets the banner?" Richard asked.

"Well," said Mr. Mancina. "This is hard."

"It wouldn't be hard for me," whispered Jason.

"Me, neither," said Dawn.

"Sh," said Ms. Rooney.

"Well," said Mr. Mancina again.

Everybody looked at him.

"Mrs. Smith's class gets the banner," said Mr. Mancina.

Dawn looked at Jason.

Jason looked at Dawn. "Peggy's class?"

Everybody clapped.

Mr. Mancina put up his hand. "There's another prize, too."

Dawn held her breath.

"Stand up, Drake," said Mr. Mancina. "Stand up, Louie.

"Your class gets the banner next week."

Drake and Louie began to jump up and down.

"These boys planted seeds," said Mr. Mancina. "Near the picnic table. We'll have marigolds this year."

"Wow!" said Dawn. "I never guessed."

Mr. Mancina turned around. "And," he said, "Ms. Rooney's class gets the banner for the third week."

Dawn and Jason began to hop up and down, too.

"Good work," said Mr. Mancina.

Ms. Rooney's class marched off the stage.

Dawn took a deep breath.

She looked around.

She hoped she'd find another mystery soon.